The SATURDAY TRIPLETS in
Teacher Trouble!

LEVEL 1 READER

The SATURDAY TRIPLETS in
Teacher Trouble!

by Katharine Kenah
Illustrated by Tammie Lyon

SCHOLASTIC INC.

**For the remarkable teachers in all our lives,
with thanks
—K.K.**

**For teachers everywhere
who make school seem magical
—T.L.**

ISBN 978-0-545-48145-8

Text copyright © 2013 by Katharine Kenah.
Illustrations copyright © 2013 by Tammie Lyon.
All rights reserved. Published by Scholastic Inc.
SCHOLASTIC and associated logos are trademarks and/or registered trademarks of Scholastic Inc.

12 11 10 9 8 7 6 5 4 3 2 1   13 14 15 16 17 18/0

Printed in the U.S.A.   40
First printing, September 2013
Designed by Jennifer Rinaldi Windau

It was Saturday morning.
The triplets were eating breakfast.

"Let's do something," said Ana.
"Something fun," said Bella.
"I know," said Carlos.
"Let's play Teacher!"

"But it is Saturday," said Ana.
"I mean pretend we are at school,"
said Carlos.

They got pencils and paper.
They pushed chairs into rows.

"There are only three of us," said Ana. "We need a bigger class."

The triplets got stuffed animals
and put them on the chairs.

Their cat, Boo, sat down, too.

"I want to teach first," said Bella.
"No, me!" yelled Ana.

"It was my idea!" yelled Carlos.
"I go first."

"Good morning, class," said Carlos.

Mr.
Carlos

"Good morning, teacher,"
said Ana and Bella.

The stuffed animals did not
say anything.

"I will teach you about farms," said Carlos.

"Farmers grow food," said Ana.
"Milk comes from their cows,"
said Bella.

The stuffed animals did not know about farms.

Teacher Ana said, "Let's work on numbers and letters."

Bella counted.

Carlos spelled.

"Very good!"
said Teacher Ana.

The stuffed animals could not count or spell.

Teacher Bella said,
"Look at the clock.
What time is it?"

"Time for lunch!"
said Ana and Carlos.

The stuffed animals were
not hungry.

After lunch, Ana said,
"We need a new class."
"One that talks and has fun,"
said Bella.

"We have one!" said Carlos.
"At school!"

On Monday, the triplets went to school.

Their teacher said, "Good morning, class."
They learned about farms.
They worked on numbers and letters.
Their teacher said, "Very good!"

The triplets had fun at school.

They talked and played with their friends.

Real school was the best kind of all!